This book belongs to

....

MURILLA GORILLA

AND THE
MISSING MOP

JENNIFER LLOYD   ILLUSTRATED BY JACQUI LEE

SIMPLY READ BOOKS

To the staff and students of McCaig Elementary. —J. Lloyd
For my family. —J. Lee

Published in 2018 by Simply Read Books
www.simplyreadbooks.com

Text © 2018 Jennifer Lloyd
Illustrations © 2018 Jacqui Lee

Library and Archives Canada Cataloguing in Publication

Lloyd, Jennifer, author
Murilla Gorilla and the missing mop /
written by Jennifer Lloyd ; illustrated by Jacqui Lee.
((Murilla Gorilla ; 4)

ISBN 978-1-927018-78-1 (hardback)

I. Lee, Jacqui, illustrator   II. Title.

PS8623.L69M876 2017   jC813´.6   C2015-902462-5

We gratefully acknowledge for their financial support of our publishing program the Canada Council for the Arts, the BC Arts Council, and the Government of Canada.

Manufactured in Malaysia
Book design by Naomi MacDougall

10 9 8 7 6 5 4 3 2 1

Canada Council Conseil des arts
for the Arts   du Canada

Canada BRITISH COLUMBIA BRITISH COLUMBIA ARTS COUNCIL

Contents

Chapter 1
Feeling Thirsty

The afternoon sun shone down on the African Rainforest.

Murilla Gorilla was taking a walk in Mango Market.

She was hot. She was thirsty. Her detective backpack felt heavy on her shoulders.

A cold drink would be perfect right now, she thought.

Murilla walked towards Leopard's Lemonade Stand.

Up ahead, Murilla could see Mandrill standing at her mop stand.

"Murilla!" called Mandrill.

Murilla waved quickly to Mandrill but she kept walking. Murilla's throat was dry.

"Murilla! Can you come over here?" called Mandrill again.

Murilla walked faster. She kept her head down.

LEMONADE

MOPS

JAMS & JELLY

Parasols

BUMP!

Murilla ran right into Mandrill.

"Murilla! You did not come when I called you."

"Sorry, Mandrill. I am thirsty. I am on my way to Leopard's Lemonade Stand."

"Murilla, you do not have time to drink lemonade! I have a case for you. One of my mops is missing."

Chapter 2
Messy Mops

Murilla looked around Mandrill's mop stand. Mops were everywhere, all over the ground.

"Mandrill, how can you tell if a mop is missing? It is such a mess around here!"

"My mop stand is not usually like this," answered Mandrill. "I made the mess when I was searching for my mop."

"What does the missing mop look like?" asked Murilla.

"It has a short handle."

Murilla took out her notebook. She drew a picture of a mop with a short handle.

"Where were you when the mop went missing?" she asked.

"I had gone to chat with Anteater. When I came back, the mop was gone."

"I will start hunting for clues. But first, do you have anything to drink?"

"Murilla! This is a mop stand. I only sell mops!"

"Right."

FRESH LEMONADE

Chapter 3
Extra Cleaning

Murilla opened her backpack.

She pulled out some spray cleaner.

"This is not what I need."

She pulled out a dustpan.

"No, not that, either."

At last she pulled out her feather duster.

SWISH! SWISH! Murilla swished the feather duster all over Mandrill's mop bucket.

"Why are you cleaning my mop bucket?" asked Mandrill.

"I am not cleaning your mop bucket! I am dusting for prints," said Murilla.

"Murilla, if the mop thief left prints, I think that you just cleaned them all off!"

Murilla was embarrassed. She needed a new way to solve the case.

Chapter 4
New Clues

Murilla took out her magnifying glass.

This time she looked for clues around the mop bucket.

Murilla stepped over a mop. Then she stepped over another mop. It was hard to walk.

"I'll just clean up these mops, so I can look for more clues."

When she lifted a mop from the ground, she found something underneath. It was a drinking glass!

"Mmm! Something to drink!" said Murilla. She raised the glass to her mouth but it was completely empty.

"Mandrill, did you leave a drinking glass on the ground?"

"No, I do not know how that got there."

Murilla put away another mop.
But when she stepped forward,
something felt sticky under her foot.
Something felt sticky under her
other foot too.

"Mandrill, did you leave a sticky mess around your mop stand?"

Mandrill looked annoyed. "Maybe the mop thief made the mess when he took my mop."

Murilla looked down at the sticky mess on the ground and then at her own sticky feet. "If the thief made this sticky mess, he must have stepped in it too."

Murilla took out her notebook.
She tried to draw an animal with
sticky feet.

It was hard!

But drawing sticky feet gave
Murilla an idea...

Chapter 5
A Trap

Murilla opened her backpack again.

"What are you looking for?" asked Mandrill.

"Cotton," said Murilla. "I am making a sticky feet trap."

Murilla pulled out a large bag of cotton. She dropped the cotton pieces on the path.

COTTON

Then she ducked behind a plant.

Mandrill ducked behind the
plant too.

"How does the sticky feet trap
work?" asked Mandrill.

"Shh. Someone is coming."

It was Anteater. He walked on the cotton.

Murilla jumped out.

"Anteater! I need to check your feet!"

Anteater looked confused.

He lifted one foot and then the other.
No cotton had stuck to his feet.

"Not sticky!" said Murilla.

Anteater shook his head and
walked away.

Murilla and Mandrill ducked
behind the bush again.

Two more animals were coming…

Ms. Chimpanzee was carrying
a shopping bag. Little Chimp
was eating something from a jar.

They walked on the cotton.
Murilla checked. Ms. Chimpanzee's
feet were not sticky. Little
Chimp's feet were not sticky.

But Little Chimp's face was sticky.

"Little Chimp! What do you have on your face?" asked Murilla.

"Elephant's pineapple jam," said Little Chimp.

"It is on special today," explained Ms. Chimpanzee.

Sticky jam gave Murilla another idea…

Chapter 6
Messy Elephant

Murilla packed up the sticky feet trap and she headed down the path.

"Where are you going?" asked Mandrill.

"To see Elephant," said Murilla.

Mandrill followed.

"Would you like to try some pineapple jam?" asked Elephant.

"Mmm," said Murilla.

"Murilla! Don't you have to check Elephant's feet?" said Mandrill.

"Right."

Murilla laid out the trap.

"Elephant, can you please step on this cotton?"

Elephant stepped on it.

"Lift your foot," said Murilla.

Murilla checked. Elephant's foot was covered jam. It was also covered in cotton!

"Elephant, did you spill something sticky today?" asked Murilla.

"Of course. Making jam is very messy."

"How did you clean up your mess?"

Elephant pointed to a mop in the corner of his stall.

It had a long handle.

"Not the mop thief!" Murilla said to Mandrill.

Murilla was tired. She was still hot. She was still thirsty.

"Elephant, do you sell anything to drink?"

"No. Why don't you go to Leopard's Lemonade Stand instead?"

"A cold drink will help me solve the case," agreed Murilla.

Mandrill sighed. She followed Murilla to Leopard's Lemonade Stand.

Chapter 7
Some Lemonade Please

Mandrill sat down at Leopard's Lemonade Stand.

Murilla sat down too.

But when Murilla sat down, the seat felt sticky.

"Leopard, why is my seat sticky?"

"I spilled a jug of lemonade this morning."

"Mmm, lemonade. Can I please have a glass?"

Mandrill poked Murilla. "Murilla! Don't you have something else to ask Leopard?"

"Right. Sorry, Mandrill. Leopard, can Mandrill have some lemonade too, please?"

"No, Murilla! Not that!" said
Mandrill.

Murilla remembered the case.

"Leopard, what did you use to
clean up your lemonade spill?"

Leopard looked embarrassed. He
did not answer.

Behind him, Murilla saw a mop
leaning on the stand. The mop
had a short handle!

"Leopard?" said Murilla.

Leopard looked at Mandrill. "I went to buy a mop but you were not at your stand. I needed to clean up my mess so I took a mop. I left you a glass of lemonade to pay for it."

"I did not get a glass of lemonade!" said Mandrill.

"But I left you one," said Leopard.

"Leopard did leave you a glass,
Mandrill," interrupted Murilla.
"Do you remember when I found
a tipped-over glass at your mop
stand? You must have knocked it
over when you were looking for
your missing mop."

"The spilled lemonade must have
been what made the ground so
sticky," said Mandrill.

Looking relieved, Leopard gave
them each a glass of lemonade.
"On the house!" he said.

"Thanks for solving the case," Mandrill said to Murilla.

Murilla smiled but she did not answer. She was too busy sipping her drink.